LOUIE LARKEY
and the Bad Dream Patrol

by Linda Kay Weber
Illustrated by Nora Hilb

Moon Mountain
PUBLISHING

North Kingstown, Rhode Island

This is for
Steve, for the support
Sandy, the original owner of Louie Larkey
And Heather, the star of the story
LKW

To Daniel
NIH

Text Copyright © 2001 Linda Kay Weber
Illustrations Copyright © 2001 Nora Hilb

First edition.

Library of Congress Cataloging-in-Publication Data

Weber, Linda Kay, 1957-
   Louie Larkey and the bad dream patrol / by Linda Kay Weber ; illustrated by
Nora Hilb.— 1st ed.
     p. cm.
   Summary: After Heather's favorite teddy bear leads the other toys in chasing
a bad dream out of the house, he struggles to get back to her bedroom
before dawn.
   ISBN 0-9677929-3-2 (hc. : alk. paper)
   [1. Teddy bears—Fiction. 2. Toys—Fiction. 3. Dreams—Fiction.] I. Hilb,
Nora, ill. II. Title.

PZ7.W3893 Lo 2001
[E]—dc21
                                    2001030907

Moon Mountain Publishing
80 Peachtree Road
North Kingstown, RI 02852
www.moonmountainpub.com

The illustrations in this book were done with ink, colored pencils, black pencil—
the kind every child takes to school—and joy!

Printed in South Korea.

Printed on acid free paper. Reinforced binding.

10 9 8 7 6 5 4 3 2 1

LOUIE LARKEY
and the
Bad Dream Patrol

Mom tucked the covers around Heather and her stuffed animals. Heather squeezed her teddy Louie Larkey. He was Heather's favorite because of his cheerful round face, lavender fur and bright red overalls. Also in bed were Nilla, a floppy bear the color of vanilla wafers, Bosley, a simple brown bear, and Zsa-Zsa, a white stuffed cat with a golden collar.

"Good night, Heather," said Mom.

"Good night, Momma. Good night, bears. And Zsa-Zsa, too."

Heather gave Louie Larkey one more hug and settled down to sleep. Soon her breathing was deep and calm. That's when Louie Larkey moved.

"Psst, Nilla, Bosley, time to get busy!" he said in the secret language of stuffed bears. He wriggled out of Heather's arms and dropped to the floor.

The other two bears stretched and hopped off the bed. Zsa-Zsa yawned and stretched. She circled and settled back down on Heather's legs. Stuffed cats, like real cats, prefer to watch while others do all the work.

Nilla and Bosley had been with Heather for a long time. They were smart for little bears with heads full of cotton stuffing, but Louie Larkey was new. His tags said his stuffing was a "newer, smarter" modern fiber. Whatever it was, it made Louie Larkey more clever than the other bears. They were proud of him. He was their leader.

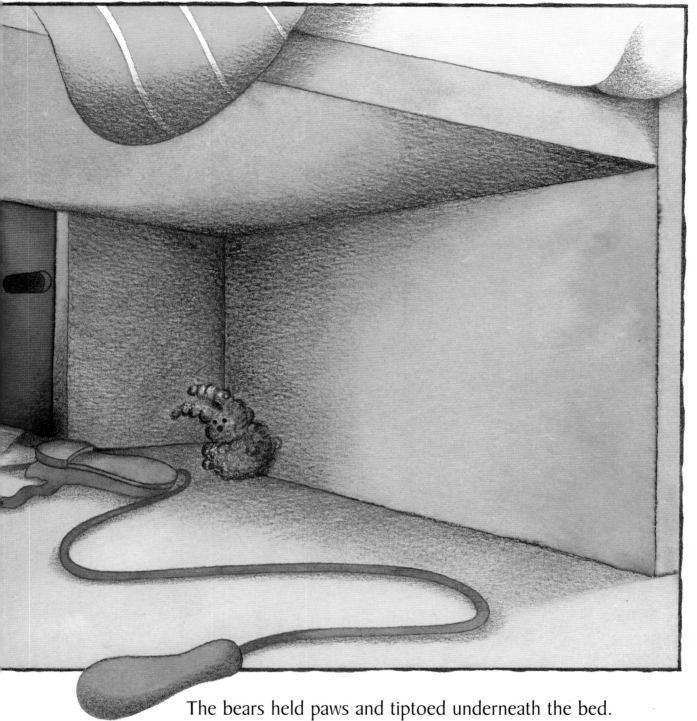

The bears held paws and tiptoed underneath the bed.
Louie Larkey took a deep breath.

"Bad Dreams, are you under here?" he said.

No one answered. Under the bed was safe tonight. A dust bunny
waved from the far corner. The teddy bears waved back.

Next they checked the closet. The door stood open just a crack, but they managed to squeeze in together.

"Bad Dreams, are you in here?" Louie Larkey said.

No answer. The bears sighed.

Louie Larkey opened his mouth to say all was clear when he heard a nasty giggle outside the bedroom.

"I found one! There's a Bad Dream in the hall," he cried. "Come on."

The bears ran out of Heather's bedroom. The Bad Dream slithered down the stairs ahead of them. They heard its claws skitter on the wooden floor downstairs.

The stairs were steep for the small teddies, but Louie Larkey didn't slow down. He jumped down the steps one at a time until he reached the bottom. Bosley and Nilla hopped behind him.

Louie Larkey waited for them.

"It's hiding in the kitchen," he said. "We've got to chase it out of the house."

They tiptoed into the kitchen. Moonlight flooded in through the windows. It was bright enough to see the Bad Dream trying to hide behind the sugar canister on the counter.

"How are we going to get up there, guys?" Bosley asked. "We need a ladder."

"We can climb up the drawer handles," Nilla said.

Louie Larkey led the way up onto the kitchen counter. Nilla and Bosley followed. The Bad Dream didn't notice them, because it was distracted by grains of sugar stuck to its toes. It licked greedily at the sugar crystals, gnawing on each claw to get every sweet crumb.

"Now what?" Nilla asked in a whisper.
Louie Larkey looked around.

"We can chase it into the sink and flush it down the drain," he said.
"If we all yell and wave our arms, we can scare it enough to run that way."

The bears crept up to the sugar canister. Louie Larkey winked, and the bears yelled.

"Yaww!" they cried.

"Yaww!" cried the Bad Dream.

It jumped up and scrambled away from the bears.

Swish! It skidded into the sink and fell down the drain.

Louie Larkey pushed the faucet handle.

Whoosh! Water washed the Bad Dream down the pipes.

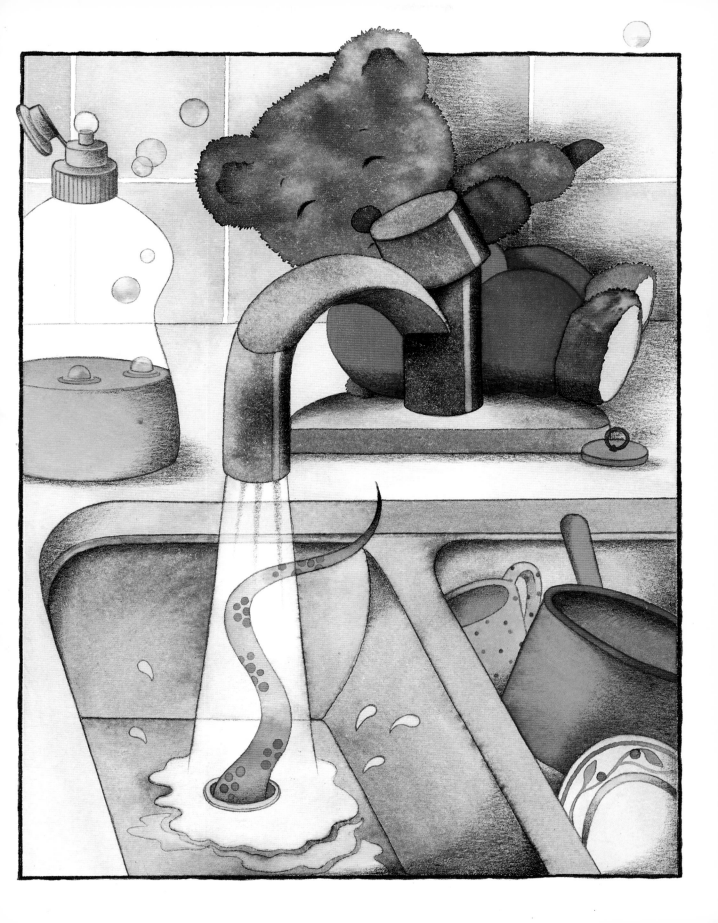

"Louie Larkey, look out the window. It's almost morning!" Bosley cried.

The sky was beginning to show a little pink.

"We've got to get back to Heather's room," Nilla said.

The bears jumped off the counter onto the floor. The good thing about having a stuffed body is it doesn't hurt to fall like that. They ran to the stairs and looked up.

"We'll never make it," Bosley said. "It'll take us forever to climb all those tall steps."

"Maybe Zsa-Zsa can help us," Nilla said.

"Good idea," Louie Larkey said. "Zsa-Zsa!" he hollered.

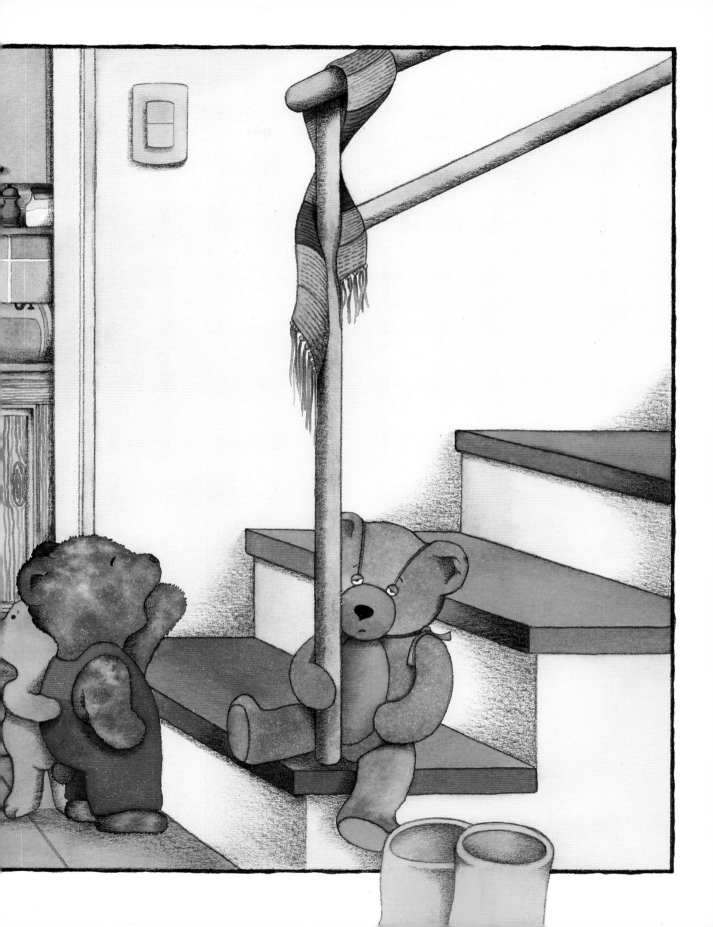

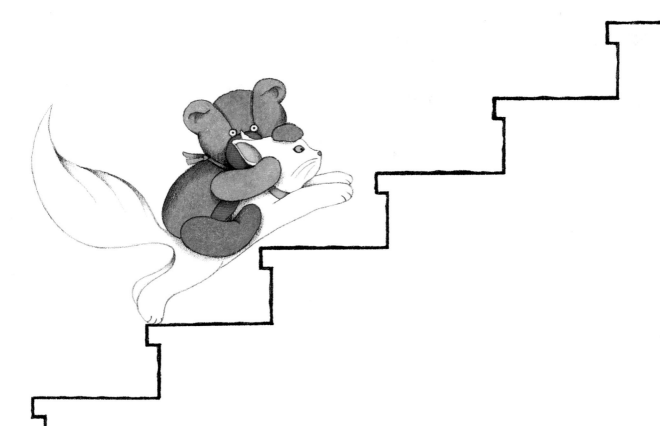

The stuffed cat appeared at the top of the stairs, then ran down like a real cat.

"I was afraid you wouldn't make it in time," she said. "What's the hold-up?"

"We can't get up the stairs fast enough," Louie Larkey said. "Can you carry us?"

"Yes, but only one at a time," she said.

Bosley got on first. Zsa-Zsa dashed up the stairs. Louie Larkey looked back at the kitchen windows. He could see pink and gold beginning to shine in. In a few minutes it would be daylight. They would all lose their magic. Louie Larkey and Nilla would not be able to get back to Heather.

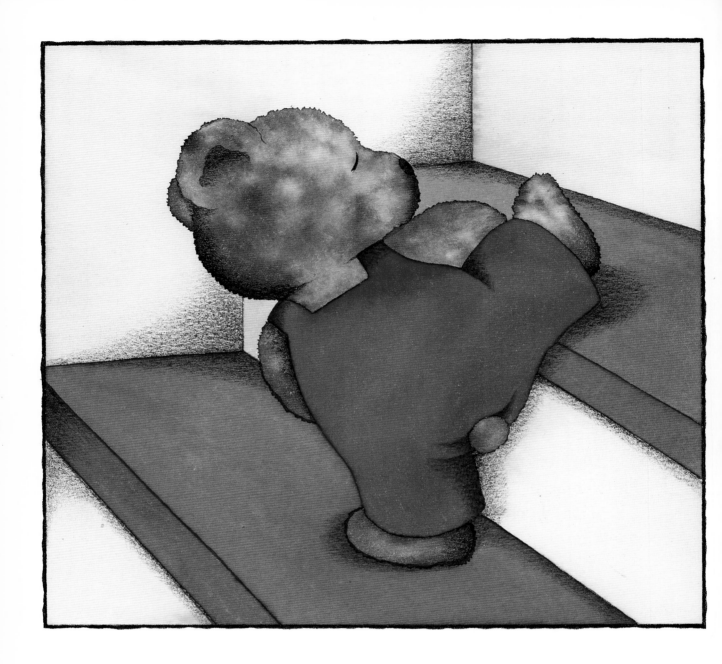

"Wait for Zsa-Zsa," Louie Larkey told Nilla, whose arms were too short to climb the stairs.

Louie Larkey began to chin himself up the tall steps. If he hurried, maybe he could get far enough by himself. Zsa-Zsa reappeared to take

Nilla up the stairs. They passed Louie Larkey, who was halfway to the top.
   But it was too late. The sun popped above the horizon, and Louie
Larkey flopped down on the third step from the top. Zsa-Zsa and Nilla
lost their magic right beside Heather's bed.

Heather wiggled and yawned.
Her eyes popped open. Bosley was
in bed with her. Zsa-Zsa and Nilla
were on the floor, but Louie Larkey
was nowhere to be seen.

"Momma! Momma!" she cried.

Mom walked into the room,
tying her robe.

"What's wrong, honey?"

"Louie Larkey's gone!"

Mom and Heather looked
through the covers and under the
bed. They didn't find him.

"Where is he, Momma?"

"Let me go start breakfast, then
we'll look some more. Don't worry,
we'll find him," Mom said.

Mom left the room.

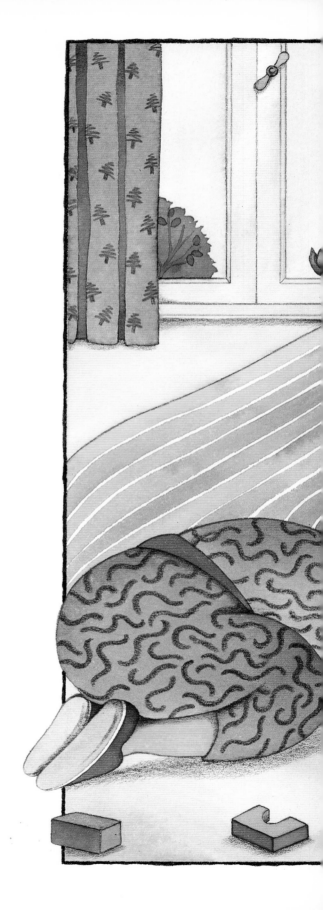

"Heather! Here he is."

Heather ran out into the hall. Louie Larkey was lying on a stair step.

"Did you take him to the bathroom with you during the night?" Mom asked.

"No, I didn't wake up. I only had good dreams," Heather said. "Momma, he must have chased a bad dream down the stairs. Then he couldn't get back to bed in time."

Mom looked puzzled. She shrugged.

"Why don't you and Louie Larkey come help me fix breakfast?" she said.

Heather picked up the teddy bear and gave him a big hug. As she followed Mom to the kitchen, she began to hum, then when words came to her she sang them.

"Louie Larkey, Louie Larkey.
Couldn't get all the way up the stairs.
Louie Larkey, Louie Larkey.
He is the greatest of all the bears!"

E   Weber, Linda Kay,
WEB   1957-

       Louie Larkey and the
       bad dream patrol.

$15.95

DATE			